The Golldooney's Garden

By
Chanmattee Lynnie Bachoo

ISBN: Softcover   978-1-5144-9127-0
        Hardcover   978-1-5144-9125-6
        EBook   978-1-5144-9126-3

Print information available on the last page

Rev. date: 05/06/2016

To order additional copies of this book, contact:
Xlibris
1-888-795-4274
www.Xlibris.com
Orders@Xlibris.com

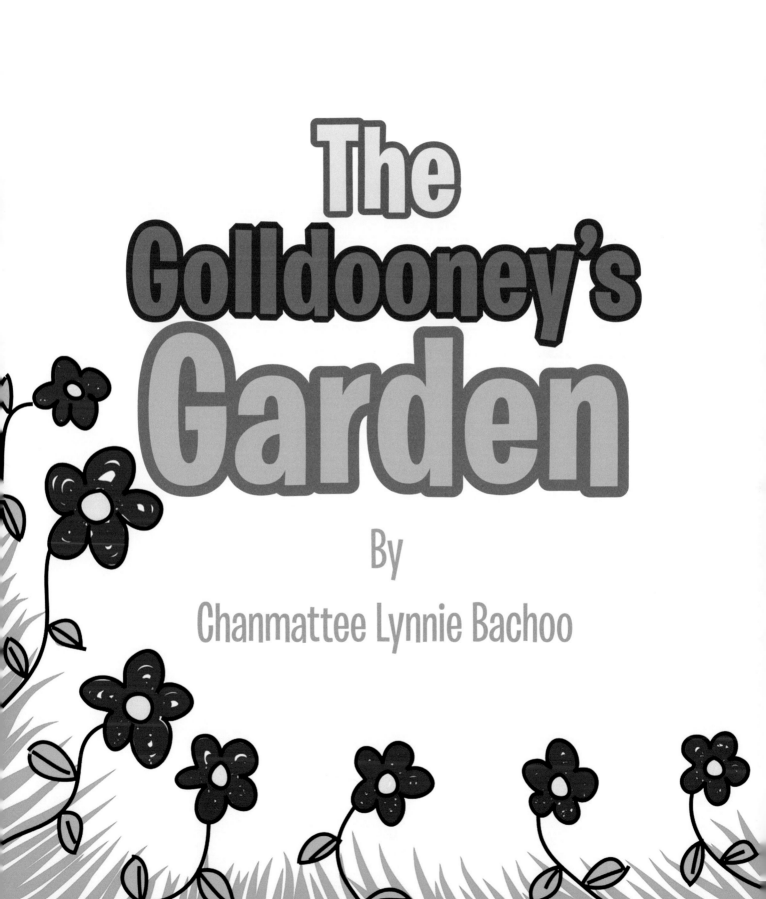

The Golldooney's Garden

By

Chanmattee Lynnie Bachoo

Once upon a time on an early spring morning there was a LADYBUG and her friend Mr. BUMBLEBEE sitting and enjoying the sunshine and fluttering in and out of each and every flower stem that they have found to fill and nourish them so they can be very healthy.

After meeting up with the other members of the bevy of about 15 Lady Bugs in her group, they decided to venture out and flutter across to the other side of the garden, where the beautiful and luscious looking Geranium flower patch and the hedges of extravagant Daisies graced the garden of Mr. Golldooney and Mrs. Golldooney. Mr. Golldooney loves gardening along with his wife Ava. Mr. Bluster Dog, their pet loves to accompany them to the garden and everywhere they go.

Mr. Bumble Bee saw them fluttering across
and decided to follow them and join the other
Ladybugs to share their meal of which was very
delictably, tastefully and delicious Nectar mixed
with morning dew drops from the night sky as
fresh as the new buds opening to new light of
scent and taste and flavor.

A conversation began with Master Bumble Bee asking one of the Ladybugs about the Melon patch that have been spreading across the corner of the gardens which was nicely lawned by the gardeners and well trimmed and shaped to suit the outlay of the garden itself.

The flowered trees, pine tree hedges and fruit trees were nicely trimmed to perfection, not forgetting the lawn that looked as green and well nourished.

Meanwhile, as Farmer Golldooney was discussing the contest with his wife Ava, the different kinds of vegetables such as potatoes, tomatoes, green beans, cauliflower which were white, purple and green, broccoli, red, yellow green and orange sweet peppers,kale,spinach, cabbage purple and green and many other nutricious, valuable vegetables not forgetting corn, zucchini and squash of all species and lettuce and cucumbers.

His wife Ava who always wore her famous broad straw hat which was nicely weaved with beautiful blue and white ribbons and a beautiful flower to grace her outlook and the other farmers and workers, were hoping that the choice of best vegetables and taste of the best foods contest for the year would be nice if they won.

The best Prize award winning for the upcoming vegetable contest which was due to take place this upcoming Spring and Summer in the state of PENNSYLVANIA and NEW JERSEY respectively.

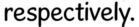

Meanwhile as Fairy Annabelle was fluttering and cruising by, she spotted three of her friends- namely Charlie Pear Feather, Misty Shea Feather and Diamond Rose Feather and not forgetting Beauty wizard fluttering and conversing with each other all by the hedges of the Golldooney's garden which led to the view of the hidden spinning of Mr. & Mrs Shimmer Spider, spinning their usual net of web catcher. They had already caught a few insects and bundled them up in their individual net of cocoons for their later consumption and was still catching and bundling more insects in their cocoons for later consumption.

What a delightful sight, when all the fairies come together, along with the birds and insects, what a wonderful and delightful atmospheric aura comes out of the Golldooney's Gardens during this time of the year.

Mr. Golldooney always goes down by the creek to check on the fresh running waters since the waterfall nearby always gets crowded by new visitors as always, and sometimes visits his garden and complements him for his efforts in gardening.

Whilst checking the creek that runs by his garden, as he is always delighted to listen to the sounds and croaking of the toads and frogs and their hopping onto the broad lily leaves in its own nature. There are many tadpoles just swimming around in the well cared for creeks of the fresh running waters. Soon they will be all grown into frogs and the cycle goes round and round.

Willowheath and the Rainbows were an array of sparkling colors brightening even the leaves and trees of the gardens. I guess that is why Mr. Golldooney won the contest for the best garden with fruits and vegetables.

As one of the Ladybugs asked Master Bumble Bee "what do you think will be the best choice for vegetables and fruits?" He replied very excitedly and in a loud voice that "there are many wonderful flavors in all vegetables and fruits and not forgetting vitamins and irons to help keep your body strong and healthy. It will be a difficult decision to make since all are very healthy and delicious in their own way and can boost many wonderful qualities in anyone's body."

Mr. Bumble bee decided to go fluttering by himself to figure out where they stand with the gardeners as to reference to the fruits and vegetables and if they will continue to produce more of these delicious fruits vegetables since he has been watching them grow all along and conversing over them when he himself flutters with the other bevy of Bumble bees who became close friends with the bevy of Lady Bugs.

We were only concerned about the
Garden vegetables, but it was later
that both bevies of Lady bugs and
Bumble bees decided to flutter across
the cabbage patches, with all the
lettuce, collard greens,turnips, lettuce,
kale, sweet peas and corn, tomatoes,
peppers, celery and all the other greens
in the garden areas, which was called
Vegetable Lane.

Mr. Wormy who was crawling on the nearby lawn adjoining the garden and who came down along with some of the cherries from the cherry tree did reject the notion that he was going to be removed. He was right, so said, so done. Nevertheless, they heard no one was leaving.

All the bevies both lady bugs and bumble bees were so happy and decided to host their own fluttering party and feasting on the nectars of the flowers and fruits and vegetables. The best garden went to Mr. Golldooney and Mrs. Ava Golldoonie and other workers in his garden. The food critic was there also to judge the best in foods prepared by some of the other gardeners which was a delight and enjoyable.

As the Golldooney's were heading to the show by train to the fair and contest of the garden's best fruits and vegetables, and best prepared foods, there were a lot of excitement travelling by train and in the open car. Bluster dog, barking and other people chatting, some playing their usual guitar music, some dancing to the old folklore songs and music.

Meanwhile, with all the bugs and bees fluttering by, the birds and animals were carrying on themselves since the contest and the winner's trophy went to The Golldooney's garden.

At Bugs' Lane, Mr. Admiral Butterfly was glowing as usual along with Ulysses and Sulphur butterflies. With Walking Stick in his/her usual upright way and the beautiful Breylline Hummingbird, complemented the choice award gardener with their beautiful fluttering and magical voices, as did Queen Alexandra's birdwing butterfly with her fluttering and landing on the beautiful flowers, not forgetting Dragon Fly and Firefly, and Grasshopper.

Harlequin Bug and Honeybee along with leafhopper and Leafcutter and our famous Japanese Beetle, and Army Worm not forgetting Ambush bug and Blueberry insects all came and enjoyed the feast and festive winner's delight.

Mr. Crow and Red Cardinal sang so beautifully across the garden each and every morning and along with many others as Mr. Acorn Woodpecker who loves to do the tap tap tapping on that tree. All the Hummingbirds fluttered by and so did the Orioles. Bewicks Wren and the Jays both Blue and Brown did their usual singing and fluttering as well.

After the contest, everyone was invited
to a picnic in the nearby fair where the
contest had originally been taking place,
and enjoy some good old fashioned
foods, and the menu was a lot of corn
on the cobs, vegetables fried chicken,
baked and grilled and all types of greens
and salads, mash potatoes, macaroni and
cheese, baked as well, pumpkin pies and
apple pies, blueberry pies as well, to suit
your delight, not forgetting the delicious
baked Turkey and fried as well. Hot dogs
and Hamburgers
and ribs were also a treat.

Master Bluster dog who always accompany the Golldooney's to everywhere, was enjoying the beautiful day and so was the other cats and other dogs.

It was a Day well spent by all.

The End.

Chanmattee Lynnie has also written her first
book about a child becoming a President of the
United States of America, which is entitled
"The Holy Grail of 1600 Pennsylvania Avenue
Zip code 20500-0003"

Printed in the United States
by Baker & Taylor Publisher Services